PERSON

a novel

ALSO BY SAM PINK

The Self-Esteem Holocaust Comes Home

Frowns Need Friends Too

I Am Going to Clone Myself Then Kill the Clone and
Eat It

Sam Pink

Lazy Fascist Press
Portland, OR

LAZY FASCIST PRESS
830 SW 18TH AVENUE
PORTLAND, OR 97205

WWW.LAZYFASCIST.COM

ISBN: 1-936383-18-7

Printed in the USA.

1

I'm walking around Chicago, feeling like a piece of shit.

It's winter.

There are many people out.

I pass an older homeless man and he is dressed almost exactly like me.

Almost exactly.

I want to stop him and grab his shoulders and say, "So I make it past 30 then?"

But he walks by me.

Eye contact is bad I think.

I don't make eye contact with any girls because I don't want to ruin their night and make them feel bad.

I make eye contact with some guys because sometimes I just feel angry.

Eye contact is bad I think.

At a stoplight, I wait to cross and there are two men next to me.

They're holding hands.

I imagine myself as one of them, standing next to me, this dipshit with an ugly face.

Later on, will one say to the other, "Hey did you see that asshole at the stoplight. Why does he live on the same earth as us, with his dipshit-ass ugly face."

And then the other man will agree in some way, if only in quiet.

Christmas music plays from someone's car at the stoplight and I can hear it through the closed windows.

Will I get run over tonight.

Is tonight the night of magic.

It's totally possible that something will suddenly kill me.

And I accept that.

I always think about getting randomly hurt and how awesome

it would be to just immediately be changed and removed from my situation.

To have something direct to worry about, like a broken leg or a really big cut.

I'd no longer be a person blending in.

When the stoplight signals to cross I wait to take a step until the other men walk away.

I don't want to walk next to them.

It is horrible for me to be walking at the same pace next to someone on the sidewalk.

And like all others, these men pass me.

Now knowing that in infinite space there is a pure negative, shaped exactly like me.

With no intentions of making friends.

Insecure enough not to make friends so as not to lose them.

There's ice on the sidewalk.

Will I fall.

If I fall, and just stay there, will someone eventually help me.

Will a police officer walk by and say, "Stay there," motioning with his/her hand to stay still.

Will I just roll into the gutter and disappear.

I don't know where I'm walking.

This is Chicago.

On a street with a lot of bars and people yelling.

Earlier I walked to Lake Michigan and I stared at it.

It remained where it was, and I stared.

No one else was there.

It seems like there and here are just as loud somehow.

It's cold and I hate everyone I can see.

All of my strength is required to hate this many people but I manage and I am proud of my effort.

I expect the same of everyone else.

No, I don't know.

I wonder what my roommate is doing right now.

Last night he knocked on my door and asked me to check the back of his neck for pen marks.

He said, "So, I think there's a pen loose in my bed and, I think I slept on it."

There were no pen marks.

I made sure not to touch his body while checking.

It seems likely that if I were to give form to what I believe is my roommate's abstraction of me, it would be some parts of a pencil eraser that someone blew to the floor after erasing something they didn't want someone else to see.

I walk by a group of people standing outside a bar and someone almost bumps into me.

I imagine myself pulling this person apart with my hands.

Just pulling off pieces of face and neck and upper-chest.

Just ripping an arm off with a single pull.

Could I accomplish that.

What would this person think of himself if I were to do that.

Would he fight it, or accept it as inevitable.

What would the people watching think.

I walk by them all and smell perfume and I am no different.

It feels like practice.

I concentrate on my heartbeat and worry it is never going to stop.

Then I worry that I will have a heartattack, and that the heartattack will hurt.

For a very small amount of time I can fully understand the pain that would accompany a heartattack, a heartattack so bad it rips my heart into more than one piece.

And I can see either accepting everything that happens, or accepting none, but in between I lose hope.

I can accept the heartattack of caring that much or that not-enough.

What if I have a heartattack tonight and say something really dumb when it happens, like, "oh jeez" and then make a dumb face when I fall.

What if that happens to me right now.

People would laugh.

I would laugh.

Oh my.

Once past the area with all the bars, there is an outdoor ice rink to my left.

People are skating there together.

None invited me.

No, I don't know, I mean that's how I want it.

And the light inside the rink is what these people use to skate.

And that light is the same that gives them to me, not me to them, because I am outside its area on the sidewalk.

My nose is cold and my nose is also dripping.

Oh my.

Nobody at the ice rink looks at me.

In passing.

They don't because it would be weird to be looking at someone this far away.

Arranged relationships with other people that technically never happen.

It feels like practice.

Yes.

Not quite a piece of shit myself, but the streak for sure.

For sure the area the shit passes over and leaves behind parts of itself.

At the streetcorner just beyond the sound of the ice rink, there is a long patch of ice on the sidewalk that I have to slide over in very small glides.

Like, I use maybe two inches per glide to be safe.

As I'm doing this, I hear my cat meowing and it sounds like he is in my coat somewhere behind me.

My cat is not there when I check.

He died a while ago I think.

This makes sense.

It sounded so real when I heard him meow, but it didn't happen.

Just the thought of my cat's ghost is enough to make me feel like there's like, a sour feeling in my head area.

I want to itch my back until I feel pain.

No, I don't know.

I see a billboard with a young girl on it.

The young girl is bald.

The billboard is for cancer research.

I feel bad about people with cancer.

I think that if I discovered I had cancer I would immediately say the word, "Phew."

Phew.

On the sidewalk in the cold weather, the word "phew" scrolls through my head in big block neon letters.

Yes.

I watch it scroll, and I approve.

It's like everyone I see now has a haircut.

Having a haircut seems like something important.

It seems defining.

I've noticed my thinking towards another person is immediately altered if that person has clearly had a recent haircut, still shaped.

Maybe that's my problem.

Cutting my own hair for years has maybe contributed to me feeling different from other people in a fundamental way.

Could that happen.

I just need to get haircuts.

Maybe that's my main problem.

I need to get haircuts from now on.

Across the street there's a bookstore and I walk to it.

I think maybe I've read here before (read in front of people on purpose not like randomly out loud among other people who just happen to be shopping).

Will they remember me there if I go in—the employees and the people there.

They will not.

Will one of them shoot me with a water pistol full of some dangerous chemical.

They will not.

I realize it's not the same bookstore.

I go into the bookstore.

Inside there is a girl walking around and she is pretty to me.

She has a pretty face and a pretty body and it feels nice to be close to her.

She fixes her glasses and walks past me, looking at the books.

I wonder if she is thinking about having sex with me.

Am I standing naked before her in her thoughts.

What is she imagining.

Am I at least present in her imagination at all.

I want to watch the imagination.

What do I look like to her.

Do I have coins taped to my stomach.

If I do, why do I have coins taped to my stomach.

That seems wrong.

I check my stomach with my hand and there is nothing there but some hair.

I say nothing to the girl as she passes.

She just passes.

And I'm intentionally looking away.

She looks at the books and I am roughly equivalent to any other inessential part of the room to her, like a corner or a tile.

I buy a low-priced copy of a book written by Karl Jaspers and then I leave the store.

When I leave I act like I am looking at something on the wall, just beyond the register.

I don't know why I act like I'm looking at something, but I know it's intentional.

I can feel that it is intentional.

A lot of times my behavior is the reaction to what I think other people are observing about me, and so yes, I am uncomfortable a lot (haha).

Outside the store on the building next door there is an advertisement for clothing.

A girl lies on a bed looking like she is dying or has some kind of sickness but still wants to fuck and the name of the brand of clothing is on the bottom of the advertisement.

I think, "So what."

I see a candybar wrapper on the ground.

I think, "So what."

Then I walk in the same direction as before.

It feels like practice.

I only cry like once a year now.

If I had a bar graph, I'm confident it would confirm this.

The right-now me only cries once a year I mean.

And it's hard to tell if I ever cry specifically about the thing happening or just because it is needed at that time.

It's insane.

I take an alleyway between two buildings.

Alleyways between buildings are some of my favorite places to be walking.

There seem to be no spiderwebs now.

And I remember that's because it's winter and some things go away and/or die.

What happens to the spiders in the winter.

I have the urge to drop from the sky and scream, "What happens to the spiders in the winter."

There's a crown spraypainted on the side of a building, and there are numbers over each spike of the crown.

And as I pass by a dumpster, I realize every specific thing I worry about is nothing compared to the main worry I have which never has an object.

The idea of haha goes into my headhole and I almost laugh but I don't because at the other end of the alley there are people smoking cigarettes outside a bar.

And it feels like everyone is looking at me, even people in cars at stoplights.

I only laugh like once a year now.

And I realize that there is nothing to worry about without first wanting to be alive a certain way.

That is somewhat relaxing to think.

If I accept whatever I get, exerting no energy for its arrival and none for its refusal, I will be happy or at least ok.

So weak.

It occurs to me I might never laugh again.

It seems possible, and also likely.

That could happen.

I accept that.

Both of my feet are cold through the shitty boots I'm wearing and I like the way the snow is coming down more now; there is maybe a few inches on the sidewalk area.

I imagine a man coming out of an alley and stabbing me a number of times until I die.

Face-down, mouth-open in the snow.

What would that change about me.

Would I love it.

Would I think that the stabbing was painful and that I didn't like it.

Does it actually hurt or is it great.

I see my killer being given a wreath and a box of candy by the mayor of Chicago at some kind of ceremony (a ceremony for killing me, you see).

And people are cheering for him.

I see myself stab-holed and crawling out of an alley to join the periphery of the celebration.

Then I hold one hand over the stab wounds and with the other hand I give the thumbs-up sign to my killer as he accepts the wreath from the mayor.

I pass more people who are out walking.

I'm on Ashland Avenue.

A lot of times when I encounter someone else out walking or running past me, it feels like we should be more united than we end up acting.

We're both outside at the same time together.

Why doesn't that mean anything to anyone.

Goddamn.

No, I don't think I actually care about that.

I thought I cared about it just now.

The word "phew" scrolls through my head in neon letters.

I feel like my eyes look really wild right now.

It's possible I have a fever.

On my side of the street there's a cop wagon with two cops inside.

Chicago Police.

The Chicago Police Department.

And I just barely resist the urge to jump and scream at the window of the cop wagon.

That would be funny and I don't think I would get arrested (not sure though).

In resisting the urge I feel something like a rush of energy through my heart-area.

Man Arrested for Surprising Chicago Police Then Slipping on Ice and Dying—Cries Wildly.

I consider walking to Lake Michigan again, this time taking my clothes off and getting in until I die.

That would work (almost sure).

I would die from that.

I'd be completely invisible in the snow and gray water and I would die from freezing.

That would work.

Plus I don't think it would be a bad way to die actually.

I don't think that would be bad.

There are usually a lot of ducks (?) geese (?) by Lake Michigan and I think it would be nice to slowly lose consciousness while they stared at me.

What would that change about their lives.

Would it cause anything new in their lives.

Maybe it wouldn't matter.

Why can't I just walk up to some people and say, "Can I spend time with you, I'm really—" and then stop.

I think about people I used to know and I wonder if any one of them is thinking about me at this moment.

That is possible.

That could be happening.

What happens when you are thinking about a person at the same time he or she is thinking about you.

I see myself before all the people I used to know, them forming a line.

I see myself greeting them each, one by one, and saying, "I really am a good person. Are we good, are me and you good."

Wrigley Field Baseball Park comes up on my right side now.

I look at the l/e/d sign out front and I expect scrolling letters to write, "Nobody likes you and you don't have a home—people just tolerate you."

For some reason then I imagine an old newscaster in front of a big microphone going, "This just in, nobody likes you. They just tolerate you."

I don't think I would react in a shocked way if I saw that.

I would accept it.

Right now I'm hungry.

I feel hunger.

A weird noise happens in my stomach and I feel bad.

The noise my stomach just made is (probably) the same like a young dinosaur telling its mother it needs food.

I consider starving to death on purpose.

Maybe I should do that.

Starving to death on purpose seems awesome to do in North America.

It would be something that people would remember.

I would be remembered as the man who purposely starved to death in North America.

The man whose stomach made those bad baby dinosaur sounds until death.

Man Found Starved, Believed Relative of a Baby Dinosaur.

I pass by a liquor store and go inside.

It smells like my closet inside.

I like it.

No one's in the store.

Then an old man comes out of the backroom, wiping his mouth with a napkin.

I ask if they sell pens.

He's confused.

The store.

Does the store sell pens.

I make a motion with my hand like I am writing and I say, "Pens, pencils."

He says no.

I walk more and come to a 7-11 store.

I go inside and ask the man if they have pens or pencils.

He says some things I don't understand and he points to an aisle.

There are a lot of people at the register and he keeps yelling at me to go different ways.

I go to walk down an aisle and he yells at me and motions a different way.

I can't seem to select the right way.

The way he wants.

Fuck.

He yells more at me and the people in line are now looking and I can only make out a blurry monster around their general area.

For some reason I smile, feeling awesome for a few seconds.

Like, I smile really hard, just watching a man yell directions at me.

This is amazing.

I laugh.

The pencils are by the back near the drink-cooler area.

I find the pencils.

There are people by the drink-cooler and one says, "Yeah, that fucking juice is fucking awesome man. It fucks you up and shit, like, the flavor."

I take a pencil to the register and wait in line.

In line I notice the pencil is the brand that is the store's name.

It is a 7-11 mechanical pencil.

When my history is written on the face of my gravestone, the gravestone that is the entire plate of stone moving beneath the earth's surface, this part will say, "Buys a 7-11 mechanical pencil after being yelled at in front of many people."

The woman in line before me is paying.

As she pays, the man at the register (the man who yelled at me) holds up a container of juice from the counter.

He says, "Go get another."

The woman just stands there.

The man at the register shakes the juice and says it again, really mad.

The woman goes and gets another.

Approaching the register again, she says, "Is it buy-one get-one free."

"Yes yes buy-one get-one."

I look at my pencil to be distracted, and I think about how the woman just blankly did what an angry man working a register told her to do, without first knowing why.

Someone yelled at her, and she did what was being yelled.

This redeems something.

No, I don't know what I'm talking about.

I pay for my pencil and the man behind the register tells me to have a good night.

I wonder what a good night is to him and then I wonder the same about myself.

It occurs to me that in order for that communication to work, myself and the man would have to come to an agreement about what it meant.

I'm too scared.

It feels like practice.

I walk nextdoor to a restaurant.

Inside the restaurant I see some people who were just in the 7-11 with me, so I walk away, and go to a different restaurant nearby.

I order food and eat my order at a table meant for four, in the corner of the place, keeping my hooded sweatshirt and my coat on, worrying the whole time that a worker will walk up to me and say, "Why don't you take your coat off."

I decide if that happens, I will say, "Because I'm undercover."

It doesn't happen.

My history is the history of things imagined and not-happened.

I eat my food without looking up and I write all this down in the white space inside the book I bought, and I try to think about an idea of the not-happened and it seems like I can do it at first but then it becomes unclear and I am not bothered at all.

And exit the restaurant.

My hood is on and it's cold outside, and I make the mistake of breathing in at the same time a long wind goes into my mouth.

Then walk home, thinking paranoid thoughts about how people are trying to fuck with me somehow and I haven't figured it out yet.

Shit is getting bad.

No I don't know.

I live in Chicago and I don't get along with a lot of people and the reasons are always new and wonderful.

2

I'm sitting in my room, listening to it sleet outside.

The room is very cold.

I have accomplished nothing today.

It feels like practice.

There's a pellet gun in my hand and I've been taking random shots at the wall.

The pellets just bounce weakly because the CO_2 cartridge is almost empty.

And now so are the pellets.

This is my career.

I am amazing.

My roommate walks down the hall.

He knocks on my door.

I don't say anything.

He opens the door and stands with his hand on the frame.

Nodding a few times, he turns and points to the back of his neck.

"Hey can you check again if there's any ink on my neck here, it feels like there is. I can't sleep thinking about it. It's bothering me. There must a pen somewhere loose in my bed and I slept on it. Last time man, promise."

I check his neck.

There is no ink.

He leaves.

I shoot the remainder of the compressed air at my face and it feels nice.

3

My roommate has been walking around in the kitchen for maybe fifteen minutes now, checking cabinets and checking the refrigerator, doing nothing.

I'm lying on the couch listening to the pigeons outside.

I've been pretty worried lately about getting cancer.

Do I already have it.

Did I get it when I accidentally touched my eye after being on the subway today and not washing my hands.

How about when I burned some of my leg hairs with that lighter yesterday.

(I burned my leg hair because I thought it would help me run faster.)

(I haven't tested it yet because it's still too icy outside.)

My roommate starts looking through a plastic bag of oranges on the counter.

"You want to split an orange again," he says. "I need something to do."

He claps at something in the air.

"Fuck," he says, "what's that, is that a spider."

"You mean do I want to split one of my oranges again," I say.

"Yeah."

"So, right now then," I say. "You're asking me if I want half of something that is wholly mine. That's what you are asking."

He walks over, rotating the orange in his hand.

"Yeah, I'm asking that," he says.

"Ok yeah. That sounds good. I need something to do too."

"Should we do this," he says.

"Yeah let's do this."

He walks back to the kitchen and begins dumping peels in the garbage.

Then he turns the sink on.

"Shit I don't know why I'm washing this," he says. "I already peeled it. You don't wash oranges after you peel them right."

I sit up from the couch and look into the kitchen.

"You washed the orange after you peeled it," I say.

"Yeah."

I brush some fuzz and hair off my pants.

"Fuzz and hair," I say.

Then I lie on the couch again, forearm over my head and eyes.

I blink a few times and feel my eyelashes against my forearm.

It feels bad.

The word "bad" scrolls across my headhole in neon letters and I see myself saluting it.

Goddamn.

My roommate walks into the living room and hands me half of the orange.

We eat in silence, kind of directing attention to the pigeon sounds, kind of directing attention to the silence.

If I had the opportunity to walk into the room and see myself there, I would point and say, "You're stupid."

But, I know I will never have that opportunity.

It seems I keep track of opportunities I will never have more than focusing on ones I do have and could have.

It feels like practice.

I look at the last wedge of the orange in my hand.

"This was a good orange," I say.

I wipe my mouth on the inside of my elbow.

"Yeah," he says. "Yeah it was."

And there is goodness in the room.

I look at the goodness and check to see if my roommate is looking too.

He is not.

Does he see it.

He does not.

The goodness hangs in the middle of the room and I take a breath.

It feels good.

I breathe the goodness into my chest and hold it there.

Feeling like I want to individually ask everyone on earth if he or she is ok.

Feeling like I'd better get started while I still have young-enough legs.

My roommate says, "Good orange."

Then neither of us says anything.

And while it's quiet I wish myself luck with everything I decide on, and I decide to wait until tomorrow to do anything.

I cough and it makes my eyes water and some drops go down my face into my ears.

4
(Other Version of 3)

I'm lying on the couch listening to the traffic sounds outside.

The tv is on and my roommate walks around the kitchen, doing nothing.

He makes a sound with his mouth that expresses he is doing nothing.

He moves some dishes around in the sink to get something out.

Then he steps back quickly when the dishes kind of fall and make a scary noise.

(The noise is very scary to me.)

I put my forearm over my head and I laugh.

"I just saw a commercial where someone falls down," I say. "On tv."

I stare at the tv and listen to the sounds outside and I think about how one day I will move out of this apartment and into a new one.

And then another.

And how I will use my most trusted moving technique.

(You start by throwing almost everything you own in the garbage or in the alley.)

My roommate walks over to me, rotating an orange in his hand.

"Do you want to split an orange again," he says.

"You mean, do I want to split one of my oranges again," I say.

He looks at the orange.

"That's what you're asking, right," I say.

He spins the orange in his hand and he says, "Yeah did you want to split this orange. It's the last one."

"Ok so you did mean: Did I want to have only part of something that is entirely mine. You did ask me that, about wanting to only get part of the thing that is mine and is the last I have of its kind."

"Yes."

"Ok. Yeah, that's fine."

We split the orange, sitting very still on different couches while we eat.

I detect some new kind of ouch in my headhole and it feels permanent.

The word "ouch" scrolls across my headhole in big neon letters.

My roommate says, "For some reason I expected there to be like, a little giraffe inside the orange when I peeled it."

"I am glad there wasn't," I say.

We laugh.

5

I don't have a bed.

I sleep on a sleeping bag, on the floor in my room.

My room is small.

I wish it were even smaller though.

Right now I can take like, two steps one way across, and three the other way.

That seems like too much.

It always seems like too much.

It would be awesome to just walk up to someone on the street and grab him or her by both shoulders then scream, "It's, always, too-much."

It feels embarrassing when I require too much of the world.

My ideal room would only have room for like, three of me lying down.

Or maybe just some kind of harness I could hang from, outside.

Yeah, but I sleep on a sleeping bag, on the floor in my room.

And I like it yeah.

It's good.

I'm not trying to be dramatic.

I like it.

One thing I don't like though is when I've worn the same socks long enough to hurt the hair on my feet and legs and ankles.

That's the situation right now and I don't like it (just being honest).

Yeah, so lying down on my sleeping bag bed I always daydream about the completely leveled landscape of Chicago, yeah.

Were mind enough, I'd have done it by now!

Cool, dude!

And you would have come across the Midwest and had to pass an empty place, me standing in the middle of it, laughing.

Cool, dude!

I can see my breath in the room right now.

It is always very dark in my room.

It is always dark in my room because the lightbulb in the ceiling fan stopped working and I am never going to change it.

I am never going to change the lightbulb for no other reason than knowing I will never change it.

There are times I still look at the fan and even try the switch, yes.

But I will never change the lightbulb and I know this room will always be really cold.

Haha.

When someone calls something pointless, and it's meant as an insult, I am confused.

No I don't know.

Another thing I don't have right now in addition to a bed, is a job.

Right now my job is lying on my sleeping bag in my room while thinking about getting a job.

Right now I am doing my job.

And I can hear my roommate walking around in the hallway.

I remain very still so he will not find me and then begin a conversation.

I have no job.

Yesterday I completed an online application for a job as a martial-arts instructor.

I kept thinking that what I would do is, I would lie that I had really good martial-arts skills.

Then I would see how long I could get away with working at the place before they found out I had been improvising fighting moves that only seemed effective but didn't actually work.

I even thought of names for the moves, and also their origins.

To the first lesson or whatever, I would wear only underwear and say that that was the traditional apparel for my discipline.

Then I would give a name to my discipline and a geographic location—probably mountainous—where I was trained.

It would be nice to even get away with like two weeks working the job because then I could maybe have grocery money for a while.

I just want to buy groceries and sleep on top of them.

Yeah.

I'm hoping to find an advertisement for a job that entails worrying when removing your hand from your pockets because you always think you are dropping something so you turn around and check the ground and shit but nothing, but maybe something, but always maybe something.

I don't know what I'm talking about.

A couple of nights ago I was in my sleeping bag bed reading and waiting to feel weak enough to fall asleep.

I heard a girl somewhere in a different apartment.

It sounded like she was trying to orgasm.

I didn't hear anyone else, just her.

No, I heard her and the bus and traffic sounds from outside and my own ears ringing (just being honest).

I heard those things too.

The girl voice tried for a while and then I couldn't hear her.

It sounded like maybe she got bored.

Or maybe she has soundless orgasms, just to herself.

That would be fucking radical.

Total containment.

I would understand that.

I want to blow up inward haha!

Your eyeballs have no bedtime because they never close their eyes haha!

No I don't know.

I like reading alone in my room on the floor waiting to go to sleep.

It's the closest thing that makes me think the word "perfection" and have the word "perfection" flash through my headhole in neon letters.

My roommate knocks on my door and I try not to move.

My heart is beating fast.

He knocks again and then leaves.

I win.

This is but one of the many victories I have exampled as a human among humans.

I have no equals.

My strength goes unmatched.

My roommate returns and knocks on my door again.

He says, "Hey man you got some mail. It looks like coupons. I'll just put it under the door here for you."

He tries to push the mail through the bottom of the door and the mail bends a lot and it takes him many pushes to get it through.

He walks down the hall and I am one person being one person again.

6

Last night at four in the morning, I went to the ice cream place across the street from my apartment and I bought an ice cream cone.

The guy behind the counter seemed really excited that I was there doing that.

I wanted to ask, "What day is it."

I judge my health now by how hard my fingernails feel.

And I find myself grinding my teeth all the time now.

7

The front window of the place I buy my dinner at tonight has this shitty-looking computer-designed logo of a man in a chef's hat, winking.

Underneath the logo it says, "Jimbo's."

The place is called Jimbo's.

And here's Jimbo, all his features drawn in circles on the front of a window, for the city to see.

It's terrible; I hate it.

And I can barely stand I'm so sick opening the door to go in.

A man somewhat resembling the logo works the register.

"You must be Jimbo," I say, pointing to the logo on the storefront window. "You have the same circle face and everything."

The man at the register wipes his hands on his apron and he nods.

"Yup," he says.

He turns and gets the order from an oven behind him.

Paying, I say, "Wink for me man."

The man behind the register winks.

I smile and nod.

He says, "Bingo, baby." Then he winks again and says, "That's Jimbo, baby."

He wipes his hands off on his apron, smiling.

He hands me my order and I hold it and I don't remember what it is.

"Alright," I say, looking back and forth a few times from my order to the man at the register. "Bye, Jimbo baby."

"Bye."

At home I eat.

When done I take out my phone and dial.

Someone answers.

"Hello, Jimbo's, how can I help you."

I can barely breathe.

I say, "Jimbo baby—"

There is a pause.

"Yeah, what is it," he says.

"Nothing man, what's up with you."

He says, "Who is this."

It's very hard to breathe.

"Jimbo, it's me. Jimbo baby, it's me. I was in before. Come on. Just—I'm calling to say, I really fucking appreciate the quality of the tomato you used in my sandwich."

"Who is this."

"Jimbo, baby, just, for real. Just listen. Most of the time when you get tomato from somewhere, it tastes like pencil erasers smashed together. Not yours though, Jimbo. Know, Jimbo baby?"

He clears his throat.

"Fuck that," he says. "I'm Jimbo baby. Believe it."

"Exactly. Not you Jimbo baby. I mean it. When I bit into the sandwich—I mean—something happened deep inside me. A detonation. Does that make sense?"

"Hell yeah," he says.

I switch ears with the phone.

"Yeah, really good," I say. "Like some slice removed from the inside of an angel's thigh you know. I kept thinking, 'How could it be this way'. I couldn't tell if it was normal reality, or something I'd transcended."

"Hell yeah, it's like that."

"Hell yeah," I say. "I expected more portals to be involved though, know Jimbo baby? I didn't know if I'd survive. I thought I had become the spirit."

"Hell yeah."

"Hell yeah is right Jimbo," I say.

He clears his throat again.

I say, "You all right, Jimbo baby?"

He tries to clear his throat again.

"Yeah," he says. "Just got this dry-throat thing going on. It's painful."

"Shit man, need to get some water quick then, yeah?" I say.

"Yup," he says. "Alright I have a customer. I have to go."

"You going to remember to get that water, Jimbo baby?"

"Sure," he says.

"Ok, bye Jimbo baby. Keep being wonderful. Don't forget that water."

"Ok bye," he says.

"Bye Jimbo baby."

I press a button on my phone and end the call.

Then I look inside the garbage can.

There in repose, the sandwich wrapper.

I touch the wrapper and breathe out, saying "Jimbo" in a half-whisper.

8

Today I tell my roommate how I've been regularly taking a multivitamin.

He tells me to prove it by punching through a car window as we walk the streets back from the grocery store.

I am holding more groceries than him.

9

I've been shaving my head for a while now.

That's my haircut.

That's the haircut I have now.

I like it because it causes people to leave you alone more.

They just assume you're a mean asshole.

I'm serious.

Try it.

It feels good.

The other day when I was shaving my head I used an old disposable razor I found in the bathroom.

I don't know whose it was.

I cut my head badly—in front, in back, and behind my ear.

There were long lines of blood coming out of like maybe four cuts.

The bathroom was cold.

And I just stood there looking at myself in the mirror, wearing only my underwear—my head bleeding down my neck and face, my hand holding a blue plastic razor with pink foam all over it.

It felt really sexual.

It felt like practice.

At one point I made direct eye contact with myself.

I laughed so hard I thought I was going to pass out.

Like, I'm thinking what if there is a secret organization of people who just make small changes in my life without me knowing it, like folding a page or two in a book I own, or putting a fingerprint underneath some clothes in my room.

What if someone is leaving me messages in small pieces of folded paper.

What if I'm actually a flower or some kind of plant but I don't realize it.

10

The grocery store I interviewed at a while ago has asked me to come to a second interview.

For bagging groceries.

They said there might be a third interview too.

For bagging groceries.

At the first interview two people were called from the breakroom when a boss wearing a headset said, "I need two team managers out front."

One of the team managers, as an interview question, asked me what I thought of as a strong quality of mine.

I said, "I am good at things."

And so I was invited back for this second interview.

For bagging groceries.

That's why I am in my room buttoning my shirt right now.

Because there is more chance of me getting the job if I don't go shirtless to the interview.

Because I want there to be a third interview and I want to be hired.

Because everything else.

And also because I remember the legal requirement of being clothed outside.

Oh my.

Hopefully I can convince the people at the grocery store that I can bag groceries with sustained success.

That is my goal.

I want to have money so I can buy food and not die.

And I want the world to see my ability as a bagger.

I want people to hear my name and say, "You mean the bagger?"

I want customers to see me bagging groceries and regain all hope for themselves because of how inspired I am.

I want people to almost faint when seeing the beauty of my ability to bag groceries.

Lastly, I want to accidentally overhear a customer talking to the manager and mentioning my ability as "swan-like."

My roommate walks down the hall.

He comes up to my doorway and stands there and he watches me finish putting my shirt on.

He's smoking a cigarette with a brand name like "Highway" or "Eagle" and he is ashing the cigarette into an empty glass jar of shrimp sauce.

I am cornered.

No I don't know.

He says, "Hey I need some help."

I agree by saying nothing.

He puts the cigarette into the glass jar and lids the glass jar and puts it on the ground.

Then he stands rigid.

"Which half of my face looks stupider today," he says.

He moves just his head side-to-side, once, still standing very rigid.

"Seriously tell me," he says. "I want to take a picture of myself and give it to my girlfriend. I just feel dumb-looking right now."

I stand there.

My shirt is almost all-the-way buttoned.

Just like a grown-up.

I touch my chesthair and a pimple beneath somewhere.

This is my destiny.

Everything leading up to right now has destined me for this.

"Just look," he says. "Just, take your time, and tell me. Which half do you think looks stupider right now. I already decided what I think, but I won't tell you yet."

He turns his head side to side to show me both halves of his face.

"I need to know," he says.

"I don't know," I say. "I like them both."

I feel doubt that I will actually go to the interview now, for some reason.

Then I almost retch because I imagine having a stomach full of nail-bitings for some reason.

That seems terrible to me.

Why am I thinking that.

My roommate stands in the doorway turning his head side to side and I finish buttoning my shirt.

"This side," he says. "Or this side."

If I ran into him I could push him down and get out of here.

Ok, so do that.

No, I don't want to—I'm scared.

Fine, do what you want.

"Both sides look so wonderful," I say. "I wouldn't be able to choose. I couldn't possibly choose. Don't put me in that position."

Somewhere someone is teaching me to another person.

And the teacher uses a metaphor involving a garbage truck that has run out of gas halfway to the garbage dump.

And the student nods.

"I just can't decide," I say again. "I love everything about you."

My roommate stops turning his head side to side and looks at the ground.

I look at the ground.

It feels like practice.

Leave your apartment.

Your apartment is bad.

Ok I will.

Ok good.

"I have to leave," I say.

I leave.

Outside, I experience a bad feeling and I realize it is because I haven't been outside for a few days so now it's uncomfortable.

On the way to the Blue Line train, I pass an apartment with a dog in the frontyard area, walking around unchained.

I stop and stare at the dog.

The dog stares back.

We are in love yeah.

It is love.

For some reason I want the dog to attack me.

Yes, please attack me.

Will you attack me dog.

Dog, attack me.

I want you to try to kill me.

I want that.

Don't be afraid dog.

Just, attack me.

The mail carrier comes around the corner down the block.

I hide behind a bush until she passes, whew!

The word "secret" scrolls through my head in neon letters and

I am happy.

My heart is beating very fast.

When she's fully gone down the block, I take the mail from the entryway to the apartment building last visited.

I walk the mail to the post office.

At the post office I buy a large envelope and put the mail inside.

I mail this new mail to the address on the original mail haha!

And somewhere, someone is forging a gold medal in honor of how I have lived my life.

I leave the post office and walk to the Van Buren Street Bridge a few blocks away.

The bridge overlooks the expressway, and I stand there and watch the traffic for a while.

Feeling like shit.

I decide not to continue my walk to the interview.

It is not necessary.

Feels good to just quit before trying.

Feels like practice.

No one is out now and I am cold on the bridge watching traffic.

Not sure what month it is but it is cold yeah.

Probably January.

And I'm still one person and I have nothing to do.

No one expects anything of me right now.

It's weird but really comforting to say that.

And it is hard to decide things.

I want badly to take off my clothes and walk down the street, but I remember the legal requirement of being-clothed.

(And plus I think I would get sick from not having clothes on).

Whew!

I don't want to get sick and die.

On the walk back I stop and stare at the same dog again.

Now, in various places in the snow where it walks, there are rust-colored piss holes.

Piss holes.

I stare for a long time and I feel discharged.

No I don't know.

I see a long version of the word "No," one with many many o's, scrolling through my ears holes, in one then the out the other and I'm the pilot of it.

Alright.

11
(Other Version of 10)

I'm standing by the front door inside my apartment, putting on my boots.

It is a cold-sunny daytime and I have to leave.

Crucial interview with a grocery store for a bagger position.

My roommate sits on the couch doing something on his laptop computer and I look at a half-filled coffee cup on the livingroom floor while I balance on one leg, left boot going on.

Staring at the halffilled coffee cup keeps me from falling.

Thank you for being there for me, halffilled coffee cup.

I appreciate you, you silly fuck.

Behind me I hear there are mildly loud vacuuming sounds in the hallway outside our apartment.

And I try not to let them scare me into staying inside.

Trying to be brave.

It is important for me to get this job.

It is also very easy for me to get scared and stay inside.

My roommate says, "Hey, you want a candy. It'll help you get the job or whatever."

He tosses a piece of candy over.

The candy hits my knee and falls in a shoe by the doorway.

He puts a similar piece of candy into his mouth and threads his fingers behind his head.

He clears his throat and says, "Careful, it has some liquid stuff inside it."

Then when I put the candy in my mouth, he says, "What flavor is yours."

Little radios on my tongue report the message to my headhole.

There are beeping sounds and I hear the message.

"It's grape," I say.

I stare at the coffee cup and we eat our candy, vacuum sounds in the hallway making me feel tired now, not scared just tired.

It occurs to me to say, 'I wish they made grape-flavored coffee.'

But I don't say that.

I don't say that because I believe he will not understand.

I watch him continue to look at his laptop computer.

And he changes the candy from one side of his mouth to the other.

Then notices I am looking at him.

He moves his head side to side so his ears keep almost touching his shoulders, making a face he must intend to be funny.

He is trying to make me laugh.

Oh.

I look at my roommate.

Just say it.

Say that you'd like it if they made grape-flavored coffee.

Tell him.

No, he will not understand.

He won't understand you.

Just tell him.

No, the statement will leave your mouth as a small void, hanging in space, growing larger at a very slow rate, until it has consumed everything, me first, willingly.

"See ya," I'll say, putting my hands on the rim of the void, taking entrance headfirst.

Just say it.

No, I can't.

Ok, if you can't then you can't.

My roommate says, "Why do they need to do a second interview anyway."

He takes his laptop computer off his lap and puts it next to him on the couch.

He sits back.

I stare at the halffilled coffee cup.

Just walk out.

Just say you wished they made grape-flavored coffee again then walk out and be free.

You want him to know that you'd like it if they made grape-flavored coffee.

So, tell him.

Tell him and leave.

No, I can't.

"I wish they made grape-flavored coffee," I say.

The room remains exactly as-is for a moment.

And the moment is large enough to slay.

I get slain by the moment.

My roommate says, "What. I didn't hear you over the vacuum."

When I don't respond, he says, "What's up, why are you staring."

I open the door quickly and run out, kind-of tripping on the doorstop into the hallway.

In the hallway my roommate becomes only vaguely memorable.

Part of a greater disliking, little different than the couch and all the other things, real or imagined.

Part of the void to be carried around.

I almost fall and hit my head on a light in the hallway but I am able to stand and the apartment door shuts hard.

My landlord is vacuuming in the hallway.

She shuts off the vacuum.

Through its detune, she says, "Hey mister. I thought you'd want to make sure to have—"

She attempts to lean on the vacuum and it starts back up and she finishes saying something that I can't hear over the vacuum.

She smiles and stares up past my area of eye contact, raising her eyebrows to emphasize something I can't hear.

It's insane.

I entertain the idea that if my present life is the punishment for a former life, then I would never want to meet myself as the self of this former life.

Goddamn.

She continues leaning on the vacuum, staring at me.

I find myself looking at the words "San Francisco" on her sweatshirt and the odd looking breasts that are probably behind.

I walk away from her and go somewhere that is an extension of where I've just been.

A bigger "right-there."

In the tiny courtyard area outside, there's a small plastic tricycle, almost entirely buried in snow.

I think a thought that is something like, "Keep track of who owes you nothing."

And I get on the train but don't go to the interview.

Instead I have conversations with other people in the train, only I don't do it out loud.

Chicago Blue Line train.

12

My roommate and I are on the small concrete deck outside our apartment, two floors up, looking out across the parking lot.

It's cold.

I only have a t-shirt on.

He's smoking a cigarette and I'm scratching my elbows.

We just saw a woman smacking her kid in the face as they crossed the parking lot.

It was beautiful.

It felt like practice.

I look at my roommate.

"Hey can I borrow your car," I say.

"Why."

There is a very long interval between sounds.

I contribute by realizing I'm pinned to it.

"I need to get some hangers from the store," I say.

"You need to get hangers," he says.

"Yes. For my shirts."

"For your shirts," he says.

He puts his cigarette in his mouth and leans back, one eye shut, trying to get keys off his beltloop.

He hands me the keys.

I go to get back in the apartment through the sliding door, but I only open the sliding door a little and when I try to go sideways through it I have trouble fitting.

I'm sideways and I can't move.

My roommate watches.

"Almost man," he says. "You're almost there."

Then, I'm through.

It hurts, but I'm through.

And I drive my roommate's car around and go nowhere.

His car smells bad.

I get on the highway for a while.

Everyone is staring at me when they pass.

I hate everyone.

Don't go back home.

Ok I won't.

All existing humans hate you.

Yes, I know.

Well then ok, keep driving so they can't find you.

Yes sir.

I exit somewhere I don't recognize.

I drive different streets in the same direction and at one point I am convinced I am the person speaking on the radio and eventually it's dark out and I park the car in an empty parking lot by an office building.

After I park I punch the steering wheel hard, three or four times and my hand hurts and I feel better.

The word "yeah" moves through my head in neon letters.

One of the windows on the first floor of the office building is lit.

A cleaning lady wears a back-mounting vacuum and cleans a cubicle.

I realize that the amount of distance between where you are standing in relation to someone else determines a lot about your behavior and feelings.

And eventually I wake up from a nap I don't remember taking.

I'm in my roommate's car in a parking lot in front of a dark office building.

I drive home.

At the apartment, my roommate is sitting on the carpet trying to get batteries into the tv remote control.

When I sit on the couch I notice how bad the couch smells.

It is a smell that in my mind looks big and formless like a cartoon cloud of two cats fighting and it laughs like a monster and it oinks too for some reason.

My roommate struggles to put the batteries in.

"I'm tired," he says.

"I took a big nap in your car so I probably won't be able to sleep tonight," I say. "Usually I can't sleep after a big nap." I make a motion with my forefingers meant to express circular motion, and I say, "One big nap after another like that."

Then I yell, "Big naps!"

"Good job," he says. "Did you get the hangers."

"Yeah they're great. Thanks again."

My roommate continues trying to put the batteries into the television remote controller.

He looks determined.

In the hallway outside, someone screams, then laughs.

Other people laugh too, walking down the hall.

"Big naps!" I yell.

My roommate drops the batteries and one goes underneath the couch.

He gets the battery and returns to work.

I slap both hands down on my legs and I yell, "Big naps!" again.

My roommate says, "You're awesome."

Then he snaps a piece back into place on the tv remote controller.

"Do you want to split an orange again," he says. "I need something to do."

"No, I'm good," I say.

He nods and turns the television on and the lights off and we lie down on different couches.

The room is dark except for the tv.

There's a show on about bridges.

A narrator talks about bridges and I wait to fall asleep, feeling poisoned by the hand of some bad magician, like, all the time yeah.

13

This is the third time this week I've sat in my room and thought about what I'd buy if I won the lottery—ultimately admitting that I'd use it all to pay NASA to rocket my entire apartment (with me in it) deep into outerspace where the sun's pull had no effect, or to where there's this other sun with the exact opposite effect on growth.

14

Something else I do more and more is I sit on the Blue Line train and I ride around for a few hours not-looking for jobs.

It feels comfortable.

I make sure to direct my sight towards my feet so I don't accidentally see a job.

It's nice to just listen to the sound the train makes against the track.

It's just nice.

The best part is at this certain point downtown. The train takes a long curve and the sun and this billboard with a funny looking frog on it both come out.

I love it!

Right now, I'm the only person in my section of the train.

There's an advertisement for a junior college along the inside of the train.

The ad features a smiling man holding books.

He looks nice.

One day I will figure out which stop the junior college is at and then I will go there and meet this man and we will help each other through life.

15

When I return to the apartment tonight, the first thing I do is I wash my hands in the sink.

Usually I forget.

Any time I don't wash my hands after riding the train and then touch my eyes in my sleep, my eyes burn real bad.

It's terrible!

I dry my hands on the couch and then I go to walk down the hallway to my room.

At the dark entrance to the hallway I almost bump into my roommate.

He's just standing there quietly.

"Hello," he says. "Did you just get back."

"Yes," I say. "You know that. You just said that because you had nothing else to say and you wanted to say something."

"Did you find a job," he says. "Anything. Where did you look today."

I put my hand against the wall, blocking the kitchen from my roommate.

And I position my face close to his.

"Yes, another good day," I say.

He stretches and uses the stretch to step backwards a little, somewhat into the darker area of the hallway.

He is looking at my mouth.

"Well, good," he says. "I knew you'd come back."

"Of course. I pay rent here."

"Oh," he says, "I forgot. I have a job for you. I totally forgot about this but I have a job for you if you want it. Can't believe I forgot about this."

I laugh.

"Oh yeah—what's the job."

"Uh I have, an opening for, someone to uh—" He sniffs, then he yells, "Eat my fucking shit."

He yells it right in my face.

He laughs and I laugh too.

And yes, we are people.

He says, "So, if you are the right person for the job, let me know."

We laugh together.

Everything looks exactly the same except we are laughing.

It is good.

I like it.

Then my roommate slowly stops laughing.

"Hey, but really though," he says. "I do have a job for you. No joking now."

I'm still smiling.

"What is it," I say.

"No really, I have a job for you," he says. "I will pay you five-hundred dollars to kill my dad. I can give you the address and a little under half of the money right now. He lives like two hours away from here." He points between us and he says, "So if you're that person, let me know."

There is a pause in which I imagine a puppy falling out of the ceiling onto my head, then landing in my loving hands.

"I'm being serious right now," my roommate says. "I will give you the money if you kill him. Make it hurt too."

He pinches at his t-shirt, scratching his chest.

He yawns.

"Hey," I say, taking my arm off the wall.

I allow a pause.

"Give me a hug." I say.

He smiles.

We hug.

The hug is somewhat long and it feels nice.

Then when it's over I walk down the hallway and go into my room and I call it a day and it calls me something else.

Sometimes I can hear my room laughing at me when I go into it.

16
(Other Version of 15)

The Blue Line train stop by my place is the stop I like the best because it smells the most harshly of piss.

There is no equal.

All the other stops aren't as harsh.

It's like, this stop has the best piss smell, because no other piss smell tries this hard to be so condensed and so—just so new.

And I get off the train to walk home, enjoying the piss smell.

I made sixty dollars doing a study on smoking after lying about smoking.

At home, my roommate is sitting on the counter in the kitchen playing a video game on his calculator.

He sets the calculator down on the kitchen counter.

"Battery died," he says.

17

I'm with this girl I had sex with a few months ago (and then now again just recently).

She lives in a first floor apartment here in the same building.

I have my head in her lap, and we are on the couch in her livingroom.

Her apartment smells like garbage, just like mine.

It's afternoon and the room is lit but not too bright.

It's nice to be with her.

My head is burnt badly from trying to shave it last night without shaving cream and her legs feel nice and cool against the skin on my head.

"Your head looks bad," she says. "Does it hurt."

"It hurts."

She leans in different directions to see more of the flaking.

She is nice to me in a way that makes me uncomfortable.

That's probably why I mostly avoid her.

And anyone like her.

"Why didn't you put lotion on it," she says. "Or like, you could've dipped a t-shirt in water and then wrapped it around your head."

"I don't think I'd like having a wet t-shirt over my head, even in private. When I think about doing that, I mean, I see myself shrugging," I say.

I wince.

She takes her hand away.

"Did that hurt," she says.

"Yes, pretty bad."

"It hurt when I touched it just now," she says.

"Yeah that made it hurt," I say. "What did you do."

"I pressed my finger into it a little. I'm just trying to fix it. Do you want me to fix it even?" She presses her finger in again and she says,

"Boop."

"That makes it hurt more. Much much more. Think 'badly,' but even more."

She presses her fingers lightly into my head.

"Boop. I can't imagine anything more than badly," she says. "I get lost after that."

I move away from her hand.

"Think of a piece of black construction paper," I say. "And like, someone jabbing a pen through it a lot, all mad."

I stare at the carpet between her feet.

"The flakes peel right off," she says.

She drops a piece to the carpet, past my face.

"Did that hurt."

"I couldn't feel it, actually."

She lets another piece of skin fall to the carpet, past my face.

"You were being a baby then before," she says.

I watch the piece of skin hit the carpet and become a part of the carpet.

"Yes I was," I say. "A big baby."

"You fucking baby," she says.

I begin to make up a song in my head.

The song is about being a big fucking baby.

She continues to peel off pieces and drop them to the carpet and I watch each piece fall.

"It's a snow-day," she says.

She drops a few more pieces.

She laughs.

The laugh is small.

It seems like she did it out of fear no one else would.

"It's a snow-day," she says. "Let's have a snow-day here. We'll stay in."

She peels off more flakes and I see them fall in front of my face, to the carpet.

This is the moment I realize that she is a real human being and I will never be what she needs to have.

This has happened before.

Another piece falls.

"Soon I will be too small to see," I say.

"Be thankful for what's left of you," she says.

I watch more flakes.

I say nothing.

Which means I agree.

Yeah, and we are there for three-million years.
Still there right now, three-million years later.
Yeah, and the room is still the same size.
And so am I.

18

I can't sleep.

I'm too hungry.

It's really late but the way the traffic is starting to sound outside my window means it's almost going to be light outside.

In my dreams now I walk through fields populated with much smaller versions of myself and they are easy to smash with my feet.

Waking up hungry is shitty I guess but it doesn't matter.

I leave my room and go down the hallway to the kitchen.

All we have in the fridge is some peppermint ice cream.

If I eat it though, I might be able to fall asleep before I get hungry again.

That could work.

My roommate is sleeping on the couch in the livingroom.

He looks dead.

I imagine a plausible series of events that results in me being accused of killing him even though I didn't, and then me accepting the accusation just because I'm too tired to fight anything.

I get the ice cream out of the freezer and put it in a bowl and walk around the apartment eating.

For a little while I check the peephole leading out to the hallway.

No one is there.

Where are the people coming to find me.

My roommate breathes in quickly on the couch.

I eat a bite of ice cream.

"Hey, pssst," I say. "Hey. Wake up."

I tap the spoon against the bowl a little.

He wakes up and turns over.

"What."

"I'm eating ice cream," I say.

Then I point the spoon at him.

"And I can see you," I say, kind-of singing.

He coughs a little.

"Do you like the ice cream," he says. "Is it wonderful ice cream."

"Yeah, it's really good. I had to tell you. You're the first person I wanted to tell."

"I'm the only person here," he says.

There's a pause.

"I'm glad you're not dead," I say.

"Me too."

He coughs more then closes his eyes to go back to sleep.

I eat some more ice cream and stare at him.

It looks like I could just walk into the livingroom and jump on his head.

It looks like me and him are dust in someone else's carpet and we can't say hello for fear of having to come up with a good reason.

When I leave the room there is just the dark quiet of the living-room behind me and I have done nothing wrong.

When I shut the door to my room, I'm safe.

I imagine a large person playing with a replica of our apartment as a dollhouse—me and my roommate for dolls.

I want to say to this person, "What's bothering you, tell me."

And I'd be fine with a million tomorrows if I could plan them all out right now and if they all began with me jumping into a large container/vat of puppies with Dutch accents.

19

A man and a woman share the platform with me waiting between trains.

They are twenty feet down, doing that hugging-swaying thing couples do when they are still happy together.

And they each have a fountain drink in their hands, hugged behind the other.

I'm watching them.

Don't let them escape.

Oh I won't.

No, I'm kidding.

Sometime in the near future, I will have no money.

I understand that.

At that point, my access to the world will lessen even more.

I understand that too.

I also understand that if there really were a force of evil, it would make sure I lived a long life, since that would mean badness for other people and myself too.

No, I'm just being dramatic.

The couple disengages from their hugging sway and the man walks up to the tracks.

He's laughing and so is she.

He pours some of his fountain drink onto the electric rails.

The woman, staying behind, she cranes her head forward.

"Nothing?" she says.

The man says, "Nothing."

He goes and stands by her again.

And the train pulls up and before it fully stops I say, "Nothing" and nobody hears.

I smell sort of bad.

20

My roommate is letting me use his car to go pay our electric bill.

We did not mail our electric bill on time and now I have to pay at city hall because otherwise it will be late.

His car smells bad and it depresses me but the fact that I am in a car going somewhere to fulfill a task that will have real consequences is enough to make me feel justified in having a day at my disposal.

I feel ok.

Pretty much the mega-champion of all conceivable tests.

At city hall, the woman behind the counter doesn't make eye contact with me while I pay.

I like it.

It's ok.

It feels like practice.

I see the word "mega-champion" scroll through my head in neon letters.

In the lobby, just before the street exit, there is a woman on a cell phone and she says, "Well then kiiiiill the bitch."

Back at the apartment, I park the car and sit in it, staring through a window into the empty laundry room downstairs.

I don't feel like getting out of the car.

For some reason, I remember this one time when I was on a little league baseball team in fourth grade.

In the dugout during a game, my teammate kicked the coach in the dick and then hit the coach on the back with a bat, and the coach was the kid's dad.

It's funny for me to remember that.

I try to smear some dirt off his windshield but I realize the dirt is on the outside.

"You win," I say. "You always win."

And I get out and walk across the parking lot.

My landlord crosses the parking lot at the same time.

The rent check is in my pocket.

I forgot to drop it off before I left.

Now, seeing her, I know I have to actually go into her office.

She has some vague expectation of her tenants, where we all act like family, rather than people with no interest in each other.

I'm trying to say she is delusional and I don't identify with her as a human.

She stops and she smiles at me and I hope in vain for a rattlesnake or some kind of poisonous snake to emerge and bite me.

It wouldn't be bad.

I would accept it.

I'm just an asshole.

It feels like practice.

"Oh hey, come on in to the office real quick," she says. "I want to show you something. Come on."

I follow my landlord into her office and she shows me a Halloween decoration she recently bought.

The decoration is a plastic werewolf dressed in felt-clothing.

It's like, February, I think.

"Sale," she says.

She bends the plastic werewolf over, trying to get it to do something.

It's supposed to do something.

Just stand still and look at the thing and wait for it to do what it is supposed to do then react the same way your landlord reacts.

Ok, I will.

Then leave the office quickly, without running or tripping.

Ok I will.

Believe in yourself.

She continues to try to get the werewolf to activate, lifting up the back panel of cloth/fur and flipping a button a few times.

Minutes pass.

During the minutes, I see the words "just walk out" scroll through my headhole in neon letters.

I see myself walking out of the office, a bird landing on my shoulder, kissing my cheek.

I see myself free and happy.

"Come on Mr. Tricky Pants," my landlord says. "Oh, here we go."

The werewolf starts to move, plastic limbs creaking.

A Halloween song comes from the small speaker between the

werewolf's feet.

The werewolf dances and mouths the Halloween song.

I immediately say, "This is great."

And I smile and look at my landlord for a few seconds.

When I leave the office, I don't turn around until I am back in my apartment.

The apartment seems unrecognizable.

Looking around, I can't recognize any of the things on the floor or anything.

It seems like someone else moved in while I was out.

Goddamn.

What if all our keys work for any apartment and we've all just been trading constantly.

"You win," I say. "You always win."

I walk back outside and sit in my roommate's car again.

It still smells bad.

That's the only comforting thing about the day.

I try to fall asleep with the back of my head hanging over the headrest.

It gets darker and colder out.

This is my backdrop.

And I hum the Halloween song to myself, laughing about the way the werewolf danced.

So good the way the werewolf danced.

21

I'm with the girl from the first floor apartment again.

I've been calling her over a lot now, because I've been getting afraid of the dark for some reason.

We are going to bed.

She's in the sleeping bag on my bedroom floor, sitting up topless with a rubberband between her teeth as she makes her hair into a ponytail.

I'm standing by the lightswitch.

I'm naked, one hand on the light, one hand kind of stretching my scrotum out at random.

Shivering.

This is amazing.

For some reason I have become the person whose job it is to turn off the lights.

I like it though.

A job.

Right now I can be confused for a happy person.

"What are you doing," she says. "Turn it off."

I look at her.

"Do you feel ok right now," I say.

"Yeah why," she says.

"Like right now, you feel ok in general."

"Why," she says.

I watch her finish the ponytail and I decide that I don't hate her, I think.

"I can't remember why I asked that," I say.

I hold up my arm and smell my armpit.

"Come here," I say. "Smell me. Do I have b.o. Like onion-style."

"I smelled you before when you were showing me that really high jumping jack. It's not onions. It's—" she pauses, "It smells more like pizza."

"Pizza sounds worse than onions," I say.

"It could be."

I lower my arm.

"People love pizza though," I say.

"They do," she says. "Turn off the light now please."

I turn off the light and stand exactly where I am.

And I half-pray/half-wish that one night once she falls asleep I can turn the light on and off, a year passing with each flash.

No I mean I half-pray/half-wish that a year would reverse with each flash.

Haha shit!

22

My roommate is sitting at the broken desk in his room.

There is a dictionary in his lap and he's about to fail looking up a word he just claimed to be real.

I'm in the doorway of his room holding the cat we're babysitting for one of his ex-girlfriends.

I hold the cat like a baby and kiss its face, avoiding the random attempts to claw me.

The cat is angry.

It's funny to me.

My roommate shuts the dictionary and sits back.

"Fuck," he says.

"It's ok," I say. I kiss the cat's face again and say, "I'm sure you really believed 'bilomite' was a word. I'm not saying you were lying."

"Yeah I thought it was like, a fossil, right," he says.

"People get confused," I say.

He yawns and puts his hands on his face like he is holding his face together.

He puts his hands down and he blinks a few times.

"Should we get some beers tonight," he says.

The cat tries to claw my eye and I move away.

There is absolute hatred in the cat's eyes.

I feel afraid of the cat.

I set the cat down and it runs away.

Down the hall.

The word "safe" scrolls through my head in neon letters.

"Should we," my roommate says.

"We could do that," I say. "Or maybe we could just buy a lot of carrots and eat them and see what that does. I think I heard that carrots can make you feel drunk too, just like beer does. We could try that."

"Yes or no," he says, scratching the back of his neck.

"Yes," I say. "Should we go to Lucky's then. They're closest. Unless you mean going to a bar. If you mean going to bar then I don't want to go."

He scratches his sideburn and says, "Fuck Lucky's. I hate that place. Fuck that place. I don't want to get shot. Plus that guy at the register always calls me a bitch. He always finds a way to call me a bitch somehow. One time he told me he was going to 'erase me.' I didn't do anything to him. Fuck those assholes." He leans back in his chair and says, "In conclusion, fuck that place and also, fuck those assholes."

"The people there don't mess with me," I say.

"That's because you look insane. They like you."

I scratch my shin with the heel of my other foot.

"Remember that old homeless lady wearing the 'Babe Magnet' hat," I say. "She used to be there a lot. I liked her."

"Yeah, she was cool," he says. "She gave me some of her animal crackers one time."

"See. Good people," I say. "Everywhere there are good people."

He ignores me.

He says, "She told me that if I eat the rhino I will have its strength and then she watched me eat the rhino cracker and she looked scared like it was about to happen."

"Did it happen."

"I don't think so but I haven't decided," he says.

I can't think of anything to say so I walk down the hall and he follows.

We put on our shoes and coats and argue about whether or not it would work to just pass a huge piece of paper around to the entire world and have people sign it in agreement to become friends.

Would that work.

What would that change.

My roommate refers to it as a "worldwide friendship mandate."

It doesn't seem convincing.

At the liquor store I stand in line holding the beer while my roommate ties his shoes.

There is a song about love playing from the small speakers behind the register.

A homeless man gets in line behind us.

He's holding a dirty plastic doll.

He smells worse than me and I smell worse than my roommate.

I establish a hierarchy.

My roommate looks at the homeless man then around the store, still tying his shoes.

"I hate this fucking place," he says. He switches shoes and says, "Why do they keep the tampons by the duct tape and the gardening gloves."

The homeless man behind us says, "In case shit gets real."

His eyes are open wide and he is nodding.

He moves his tongue around his mouth, over two big teeth on top that look like tusks.

I nod upward once and say, "Nice tusks, man."

The homeless man clutches his plastic doll closer to him.

"Don't touch me," he says. "Do not, fucking, touch me." He laughs hoarsely, then coughs a little. He says, "Pretty soon everyone will have a better chance at falling into the pile. You know, I saw the plane crash in my dreams and it was boo-tiful. It was boot-iful."

He kneels down and bows his head while holding up the doll.

"Boo-tiful," he says.

I decide to play the disappearing game, where I try to see how completely I can be gone from any interaction.

The problem with this game is that with victory comes no recognition.

So I pay for the beer and the guy at the register holds up a red plastic chip I must have accidentally given him with some coins.

He says, "We don't take bingo chips, bitch."

He flips the bingo chip to the counter, where it bounces then lands on the floor.

I grab it off the floor and take our beer off the counter.

My roommate says, "You never told me you played bingo."

"It was a long time ago," I say. "I've changed."

The homeless man shakes the doll at us as we leave.

It looks evil to me in the fluorescent lighting.

The bell on the door rings when we leave.

It is really cold out.

We walk home in the cold.

And I see Christmas lights still hung in a high-up window on an apartment building.

There is no talking.

The word "ouch" scrolls through my headhole in neon letters.

I feel concerned that knowing how to really forget something is a talent learned too late.

We get back to our apartment.

In the hallway outside our apartment, I hold the beer while my roommate gets out his keys.

"Hey, would you sign the paper," he says.

"What."

He turns the key and opens our apartment door and he says, "The piece of paper that would make everyone agree to be friends. Would you sign it."

"Fuck that," I say.

We stand in the hallway.

The door to our apartment is open to us.

I adjust the beer in my arms, uncomfortable.

I say, "I think like, whenever the next time somebody buys something off me, and they want to know how much it costs, I'm going to be like, 'Fifty clams.' And then wait a second and say, 'Actual clams.'"

My roommate is looking into the apartment.

"Sounds good," he says.

I adjust the beer again.

"You aren't listening to me," I say.

"Yeah, I know. I just kind of feel shitty."

And he is the winner.

We go inside.

23

(Other Version of 22)

When we get back to our apartment building we stand in the hallway.

I adjust the beer in my arms and I say, "I don't have my keys with me."

My roommate gets his keys out.

He says, "Hey would you sign it."

"Sign what."

He turns the key and opens the door.

"The piece of paper that would make everyone agree to be friends," he says. "Would you sign it."

I say, "I'd have to see who else signed it."

We stand outside in the hallway, looking into the open apartment.

My roommate says, "Me too."

And we stand there staring.

We are the maggot philanthropists.

"Are you going to go in," I say.

"I was going to wait to see who else would," he says.

"Ha ha," I say. "I love you."

He nods toward the open door and he says, "Love you too."

I say, "We are both winners here."

We go in.

My dinner is a handful of mints taken from the entryway of a restaurant on the walk home.

I have fun.

24

It's nighttime.

I'm sitting in the empty bathtub in our bathroom, fully clothed.

I've been reading one of my roommate's old yearbooks from like his freshman year of highschool.

He keeps it in the bathroom for some reason.

There are many people in the yearbook.

I touch the people's faces with my fingers.

I read about fun dances and experiences.

I read about science contest winners and sports things.

The word "distance" flashes through my headhole on loop, in buzzing neon letters, and I sit there.

The pictures seem so beautiful to me.

There is no relief from the feeling of the beauty of the yearbook pictures.

Goddamn.

I bite my nails and I write letters to the people in the yearbook, but I only write them in my head.

It feels good.

It feels like practice.

Overall, I am comfortable.

I'm celebrating my new status as the master-champion of the entire galaxy.

And I know that when I run from something, there is a bigger part of me that hopes I get caught than there is that hopes I get away.

My defense is that I taste horrible.

That's my defense.

My roommate knocks at the bathroom door.

From the other side, he says, "Did I leave a shoe in there. If it's in there, can I get it."

I see no shoe.

25

The girl on the first floor hasn't had a job for a while either.

She invited me over tonight.

It's too cold to sleep in her room so we sleep in the livingroom on the couch pullout bed.

The pullout bed smells bad to me.

Maybe she is thinking the same about me.

Who knows!

We lie down together and our only light comes via tv, where a friendly old man is trying to sell necklaces.

At the bottom of the screen there is a phone number and a counter.

I watch the counter while she adjusts the sheets on the pullout bed and distributes them evenly between us.

She always does that.

It's nice.

"It's much warmer out here," she says. "Why is it so cold in my room."

I ignore her, watching the counter rise.

What's the counter for.

The word "intriguing" scrolls across my headhole in neon letters.

Maybe that's the amount of friends the old man has.

Fuck yeah.

You know what, I'm one of them.

I am part of that bigger number.

He just looks so friendly.

The old man I mean.

We could do everything together.

We could go bowling together.

We could dress alike.

Me and the friendly old man, we could have dates.

Try on necklaces.

Play catch with a football.

I'd always make sure to just loft the football so I wouldn't destroy his little old-man arms.

What a good guy I am.

What a good guy he is.

I understand now why the counter is rising.

Yes.

Yes this makes sense.

What doesn't make sense is how the counter on the screen isn't exploding.

Like, I'm surprised it doesn't just begin to ascend rapidly and then melt.

"I think he just winked at me," I say.

"What."

She turns over a little.

"The old man winked at me," I say. "And it's because we're friends."

She looks at the tv and scratches her nose with the knuckle of her forefinger.

"There's no way they're selling that many necklaces," she says. She turns back to me and she says, "Hey remember that magician we saw the other day on tv. He was so good. It makes me think like, maybe some of his stuff is real."

We are quiet.

We watch the tv.

This is magic.

The counter continues to rise and the old man continues to smile, holding necklaces.

And I realize I have never once actually been happy in my life.

And also never felt any kind of care that didn't threaten to give up when challenged.

"Man, I just remembered when I was in like, kindergarten," I say. "Me and a bunch of other kids were in the plastic playhouse thing during inside recess. We were reading a book. I was always the guy who read for some reason."

"That's funny," she says.

I swallow and cough.

Then I continue.

"My best friend in class, he was this black kid named Ernest. And while I was reading, I stopped at one of the pictures and pointed at the black kid in the picture. I said, 'Hey look there's a little nigger one in here.' And like, I didn't even know what it meant. I just knew I'd heard other people say it. So it didn't make sense to me, but then when I looked at my friend Ernest, he looked so hurt. Like he already knew what that meant. Like, I didn't even realize it, but then I did. The look on his face was—he looked like he was mad at himself for being my friend. It felt stupid and terrible. Man. It's fucking shitty I think. I feel really stupid and bad when I think about myself in situations like that."

When I'm done talking I just want to keep talking so there is no quiet.

But I don't.

She gets on her elbow again and looks at the tv.

I can see part of her nipple down her shirt.

The word "sex" scrolls through my headhole in big neon letters.

"I don't know," she says. "Maybe they've sold that many. They could've sold that many. How many people buy necklaces at night though."

I stare at the ceiling, on my back.

"Shit," I say. "In that same class I had my first sexual experience. I was like, standing in line to get my homework checked and Ernest elbowed my arm and when I looked up I saw the teacher bending over. I could see her tits pretty good. The feeling was like, 'I'm alive.' That was a pretty significant class for me now that I think about it. I learned a lot then."

She turns to me like I have just happened.

She says, "Huh I remember my kindergarten teacher used to tell us about how he worked at like, some industrial job once and how he'd have black crust in his nose at the end of the day and then he'd have to scrape it out with his fingers every night. I remember that scared me—when I'd think about him doing that."

I watch the number rise on the counter.

And imagine the same counter for me, but it goes into the negatives.

Win.

The old man holds the necklaces in his hand, still talking, still smiling.

"He amazes me," I say.

We both watch.

We are not touching or communicating.

I like it.

It feels real to me.

It feels like practice.

26
(Other Version of 25)

We sleep on the pullout bed tonight because her room is too cold.

The building is always very cold.

We lie on the pullout bed together and we do not touch or communicate, watching a shopping channel on mute.

She looks at the tv and she says, "I will agree that he is a cute old-man."

I lean over the edge of the bed and reach to the floor.

"See," I say. "He is absolutely adorable and he is tremendous."

"Why tremendous."

"I don't know."

I take my phone off the floor and I alternate between the tv screen and my phone, dialing.

Someone answers.

I focus.

"Hi," I say. "Hi, is this the necklace channel. Ok. I was wondering if I could talk to the beautiful old man who is looking at me right now with a necklace in his hand. Ok. Sure."

I push a button on my phone and put the phone back down on the ground by my pants.

"Think I'm going to shut off the tv I'm tired now," she says.

She shuts off the tv and lies down against me.

"Goodnight," she says.

"I don't give a shit about you at all," I say.

We both laugh and it feels good.

It feels like practice.

"Good night," I say.

27

I have agreed to go to a birthday party tonight for someone I don't know, because my roommate wants to have sex with the birthday girl and he is too afraid and awkward to go to the birthday party by himself.

(And also because I am a humanitarian.)

The birthday girl lives in an apartment building across the parking lot from our apartment building.

On the walk over, my roommate tells me she refused to have sex with him before because, "He didn't have abs."

He kicks a rock.

"And she's fat too," he says. "So what the fuck."

I say, "If she wants abs, she will gets abs, and you fail. You have to be ok with that. Don't make it her fault."

We manage to kick the same rock across the parking lot, over ice and some areas of snow too.

And we manage because we try.

At the birthday party, there are people all around me and it feels un-good.

Like heat, somehow.

No I don't know.

I sit on the couch looking straight ahead.

This is my etiquette.

I am proud of how good I have become at calmly not participating in things.

The birthday girl comes up to me and introduces herself and then she starts rubbing my shaved-head, stopping only for a second to fix her birthday hat.

"Can I do this," she says.

"It feels terrible to me," I say. "But happy birthday."

"Thanks, can I do this."

She keeps rubbing my head.

It feels bad at first yes but then I notice that I'm getting a danger-ously fast hardness in my dick area.

Magnet fast.

Dangerous!

Her boyfriend comes over and they walk away together, him looking at me.

He probably wanted to rub my head.

Later on, when I'd really accomplished a good feet-stare, this girl starts falling all over the apartment, yelling about how she is Korean.

She falls over to a person and yells in his face, "I'm Korean!"

Then she does it again with another person.

The apartment is small enough that everyone heard it the first time I think.

I'm pretty sure she accomplished her communication with the first try.

But she keeps telling more people.

She walks all over the apartment yelling that she is Korean.

And for a finale, she falls over behind my back onto the couch, into immediate sleep.

There's another person sitting next to me on the couch.

He is someone I don't know and he is rolling a cigarette and he is looking at it.

He laughs.

"She went from yelling to sleeping faster than anyone I've ever seen," he says.

"There's still hope for people," I say.

I pick her head up and put a pillow beneath.

"Don't touch me," she says, mumbling, "Or I'll punch your skull off I'm Korean."

I brush her hair behind her ear with my hand so her hair won't get in her mouth as she's threatening me.

I want to see and hear the threat.

And I sit on the couch, looking at the sleeping Korean girl.

A little bit later, my roommate and I leave and we manage to co-operatively kick another stone from the birthday girl's apartment all the way back to our apartment.

It is amazing.

Once back, we stand just inside by the dark entryway taking our shoes off.

My roommate locks our door.

"See you tomorrow," he says.

I say, "I know."

Then he goes to bed and I go out the backdoor to the deck.

I stand on the deck.

It's very cold out.

There's a color and ringing to the sky that lets me know it is close to morning.

I look at the clouds and I feel uncomfortable.

The word "humongous" scrolls through my headhole in neon lettering.

28
(Other Version of 27)

The sun's coming up and my roommate and I are standing on the deck.

We just returned from a birthday party for some girl he kind-of knows.

He has a cigarette and he is looking at where the sun is appearing.

"This isn't so great," he says.

I agree by saying nothing.

He finishes his cigarette and puts it out against the bottom of his shoe.

After a very long silence, he says, "Getting older means you have less and less fun."

I agree by saying nothing.

I have the type of cold feeling that makes your chest muscles, like, bubbly.

Hope I don't get sick and die.

The dream I have when I go to sleep involves me crawling through a very narrow wooden corridor for a very long time.

29

I can't sleep.

My room is cold and for some reason I'm scared to leave.

I want to leave.

The words "death penalty" flash through my headhole in neon letters.

This will never end.

Just go to sleep.

Try again tomorrow.

You are a champion.

No, get up and get some cereal.

Yes, that will help you occupy time.

Ok I will.

Ok good.

My phone rings and it is the girl from downstairs and I don't answer.

I don't know what time it is or the date.

I leave my room and walk to the kitchen to get a bowl of cereal.

In my biography this will be the defining event.

This will be the part where I ascend to control.

My roommate's box of cereal is on the counter.

I take some.

While pouring, I worry.

This is bad.

My roommate will know.

The box will feel less heavy to him.

No.

No maybe not.

No he'll have to know.

How could he not have an approximate understanding of how much his box of cereal currently weighs.

Ok I'll just have to put a trail out of the apartment to another apartment so he'll think someone else took them.

Perfect.

This is perfect.

Yes.

This is good.

I will do this.

When I go to pour, dry cereal spills on the ground.

The plastic bag has been incorrectly opened.

The cereal pieces tap the ground, crushed by my attempts to dance away from them.

Ruined!

I think about just kneeling in the kitchen and screaming, "Fucking ruined!"

It seems rewarding.

Thinking also about walking outside and randomly kneeling and screaming, "I'm ruined!"

Instead, I leave the cereal on the counter and go back to bed, no longer excited about being myself.

Not excited about being fertile either.

Not really excited about some other things that have names if I really think about them too.

And I have one long word in my head that is millions of words bent together.

The giant word laughs at me whenever it wants.

And no, there is no such thing as a weekend when you don't do anything during the week.

And yes, I want something definitive to happen.

I think tomorrow I'll burn myself on the stove so people will feel sorry for me.

Not sure.

It seems like you just have to have an idea about where you are going and that makes things better.

My feet are too cold to sleep maybe that's it.

And all my socks are gross—too gross for me.

This is the defining moment, when I have enough self-esteem to say yes to better socks and better hygiene.

Goddamn.

30

It's morning and the girl on the first floor has an actual bed and I am pretending to sleep in it.

She has her arms wrapped around me, kissing my back.

I think I have acne on my back.

Goddamn I hate myself.

She's been awake for thirty-eight minutes, trying to wake me up so I'll have sex with her.

I know thirty-eight minutes have passed because I have been facing the alarm clock the whole time, opening my eyes randomly to check the time.

Time is the slowest when you're pretending to sleep.

I forgot to brush my teeth last night.

My mouth tastes like there's shit in it right now.

Whenever I push on this one molar with my tongue, it tastes like, some kind of shit-plant is sporing.

I'm really worried about how much I keep forgetting to brush my teeth.

I think it's because my roommate buys bubble-gum flavored toothpaste.

And I always want to swallow it right away.

And every time I swallow it, my stomach really hurts.

Like really hurts bad.

Like it gets so cramped I can't stand sometimes.

The toothpaste fizzes up right away too.

Fuck.

I don't know why I am so upset about the toothpaste but I really really am.

The girl next to me stops kissing my back and she gets up and leaves the room.

When she is fully gone from the room I open my eyes and stare at my boots, near her broken closet door.

The words "You are a pussy" scroll through my headhole in neon letters and it makes sense.

And I sit there and eat it.

I scream in my head.

It takes forever.

Things outside the apartment building are moving and making sounds.

The sounds make me jealous of something I can't picture.

I just want to go outside and never come back.

Go into the sounds.

I get up and put on my underwear.

In the kitchen, I look at the ground and the word "dumbass" forms in the tile.

The word "dumbass" laughs at me, and the laugh is mean-sounding, evil.

"Good morning," she says.

"Thank you."

She hands me a cup of water and we stand in the kitchen together and I try to think of something that is going exactly right.

There has to be something right now that is right—that exists as anyone would want it.

We make no eye contact.

Her and I.

We get along.

"Will you go to the store with me," she says.

"What," I say, even though I heard correctly.

We're silent some seconds more.

Then some seconds more.

And these seconds see the deaths of other seconds, see new relationships formed by some random act of binding, see many others through the same silence.

"What," I say, again.

I have an urge to throw my cup against the wall.

I don't though.

I don't because I know I will sit there and pick up every piece out from the carpet.

Just leave.

Leave her apartment.

Ok.

I pour the water out in the sink and then I finish dressing and leave.

Outside I feel very stupid.

Like the air is effecting a bad chemical reaction with my skin and face.

Everything looks unfamiliar.

There's nowhere to be.

I walk to a park a few blocks away and sit on a bench with my hands over my ears.

It's cold out.

In some ways it is the best moment of my life.

In some ways I am always telling the truth.

31
(Other Version of 30)

I leave her apartment and go to the park nearby.

I sit on the swingset at the park until I'm really cold.

Eventually, a homeless man walks up to the metal garbage can by the swingset.

He looks through the garbage can.

Then he takes out some old chicken legs and eats them.

I watch him eat the garbage.

I want to say, "Pass that shit dude."

But I feel too shy.

He comes up to me and searches both his pockets, holding a chicken leg in his mouth.

He takes out two plastic dogs.

"Want a dog," he says carefully, lips around the chicken leg.

"How much man."

"Whatever you give me," he says.

I give him almost a dollar in change and I take a small plastic dog.

I secretly name the dog, "Mega-Dog."

The homeless man takes the chicken leg out of his mouth with his pointer finger and his thumb, like a cigar.

He looks at the other plastic dog in his hand.

I notice.

"I'm breaking up a marriage," I say.

He laughs.

"You awful," he says.

He keeps laughing and he goes back to the garbage, takes out more things.

I see the words "good job" scroll through my headhole in neon letters.

And I feel like the mayor of a small room with no one else in it.
I leave the park and walk.
And I decide I don't like waking up.
And I decide I want to walk in a straight line until I am very far away, but I also know every straight line walked is a commitment and every straight line is many other straight lines and they intersect and sometimes they overlap completely.

32

I haven't slept in two days so I feel tired now, lying on my sleeping bag.

My feet are very cold but I am ok.

In the long transition to sleep I entertain a complex paranoia about a group of people who will be assigned to review each action I have taken throughout my life.

And once dead, I'll meet them in council.

There will be a group assigned to review my "thank-yous said" to "those not said."

There will be a group assigned to review every face I've made just after waking up.

There will be a group assigned to review how I treated people who asked me for help.

And a group assigned to review the times I felt bad but didn't tell anyone.

A group assigned to review the times I deliberately threw crayons into the small fan my third grade bus driver positioned by his face.

And a group assigned to review bugs I needlessly stepped on.

A group for this nap I'm taking too.

And in the paranoia, I see myself getting dressed-up to go before them and answer questions.

I'm very nervous before each council but I try to be brave.

"This nap you took—" someone says.

"Yes?"

A mean-looking woman in the middle of the panel, she clasps her hands together and she says, "Tell us about this nap."

When I wake up, one of my legs is numb.

And I remain awake in my sleeping bag, staring at the blinds until the black behind gets more blue, then lighter blue, then white.

Sometimes I definitely feel a sense of accomplishment but it's never after accomplishing something.

33

My roommate and I are driving home after buying paper towels for the apartment.

A slapping sound happens against the bottom of the car and I look over my shoulder through the back windshield.

"You just ran over a cardboard box," I say. "Looks like it had already been run over though, so you're good."

He switches hands on the steering wheel and he says, "Thanks for telling me. Keep me notified."

I drum on my thighs.

"I will," I say.

Then I look down at the new boots I am wearing.

I went for a walk a few days ago and the entire bottom part of my right boot came off and like, I fell into the street.

It was really fucking pathetic.

A car almost hit me.

I think the driver saw me there lying in the street, pathetically holding up my leg to show him the flappy boot, and just forgot about continuing to swear and yell at me.

So dumb.

When I got back to the apartment building, this old man down the hall gave me another pair of boots.

He's always outside smoking thin cigars and when he saw my boots he gave me a pair he never used.

I wanted to make a card for the old man that had two birds on a branch and beneath the picture it would say, "Good people tend to branch out."

But I didn't.

I just took the boots.

My roommate puts on the turn signal and turns.

I smell something strange in the car for a second and then I don't.

I would call the smell "leafy."

It's insane.

I look over my shoulder through the back windshield.

"Hey you just ran over a plastic bag," I say.

"So what," he says.

I settle in my seat.

"So just another victim," I say. "When will it end."

"I can't stand myself," he says.

It sounds rehearsed though.

I laugh for some reason.

I definitely want to get better about not doing things I don't understand.

At a stoplight, my roommate takes a leaf off the dash and drops it over his shoulder to the backseat.

He seems very nervous.

He says, "We have to stop by the video store too so I can drop off a video." He clears his throat and says, "I just wanted someone to come with me man. Sorry to trick you, but I can't do things like this alone. I'm sorry I tricked you but please, don't leave me now. Don't make me go alone man. I was honest at least. I was honest with you. Note that."

"This will not be forgiven," I say.

We pass a small billboard that reads, "Embryos are babies too."

"Embryos are babies too," I say, watching the billboard go behind us.

"Oh yeah."

"Yeah," I say.

He says, "How about cars, are cars babies too?"

"I think so, yeah," I say. "Or wait, no. No, cars aren't babies. Cars have motors and babies don't."

He lifts his eyebrows, still watching the road.

"Babies don't have motors. You don't think so?"

"No man. Pretty sure," I say.

"Unless you consider the heart a motor," he says.

"Which I don't."

My roommate straightens himself in his seat and puts both hands on the steering wheel.

"Ok," he says, "what about roads, are roads babies too."

I think about it.

About a hundred feet up in the air, I see a purple balloon, lost and going higher.

I laugh, watching the balloon over my shoulder as we pass.

The word "brother" flashes across my headhole in neon letters.

"Uh, no," I say.

"Yeah you're right," he says.

"See. Only embryos are babies too."

We pull up to the video store and my roommate slows the car.

"Just throw the movie by the drop box from here," he says. "It'll be close enough. I don't feel like getting out."

I lean out the window.

I throw the video out and I say, "There we go."

The video case hits and slides along the blacktop a little.

I lean back into the car.

My roommate says, "You are my brother."

"And you are mine."

We drive away.

I don't know what time it is at all, like even within an hour.

And I'm thinking a thought that is something like, "Be thankful for what's left of you."

"So how about embryos, are embryos babies too," my roommate says.

"Yeah that was the first thing the billboard said. Do you remember that."

He laughs, like he's unsure how to respond.

We drive past buildings I recognize and some I don't and I think about the happiness I would feel if I fell asleep and woke up and we were entering a state three or four states away.

35

I have maybe a hundred dollars left in my bank account and today I leave the apartment and walk to the bank to withdraw it.

I just want to see it.

I just want to have it in my hands and then hit myself in the head with it.

In the parking lot outside my apartment building, I see my landlord leaning inside her car, cleaning it.

She comes out of her car when I pass.

"Are you happy at all," she says.

She squints then pushes her tinted eyeglasses up with her finger.

"Not really," I say.

Then I shake my head, to confirm that I don't think so.

"No, not at all. You're not," she says. "Are you having fun though," she says, squinting with her hand over her eyes. "Are you having fun at all."

"Yes, definitely," I say.

She smiles.

"Ok, that's all I want to know," she says.

She spits her gum into a puddle by her feet.

"Things are going nowhere for you," she says.

She closes her car door.

"No-way-yer," she sings, walking away.

The walk to the bank is nice.

It feels nice to walk.

In the lobby I go to the teller window with the most attractive person in it.

"I want to take all my money out," I say.

"I want to take you out," says the person at the window, winking at me and running her thumb across her throat. "Here, take this form."

I fill out the form and I walk out of the bank with all my money. 84 dollars.

And for some reason, in the parking lot out front, I worry that an eagle will swoop down and fly away with my money.

That is why I fear the eagle I guess.

There's a homeless man pushing a shopping cart near the bank's drive-through.

I've met him before.

He used to sell gym socks by the 90/94 highway entrance ramp.

He's cross-eyed.

He told me he'd fought in the war.

When I asked which one, he said, "All of them."

He pushes his shopping cart and I start to walk across the shopping area to avoid him.

Across the parking lot from the bank there's a small jewelry store.

The store is small, not the jewelry I mean.

I go in.

I have the jeweler show me things that cost around 84 dollars.

Necklaces.

"All these are around that amount," he says, motioning over the glass counter. Then he motions up and down on himself and he says, "And all this is around priceless, sweetheart."

I laugh and nod.

I point to a necklace.

"Ok," I say. "I'll buy that one."

"Which one."

I lean over and point again.

When I lean, I can smell my armpit.

It seems like the jeweler smells it too because he looks at me like, "What have you done, you sick asshole."

The word "death" flashes through my mind in neon letters.

I see myself saluting it.

I see the right way to do everything but I can't memorize any of it quick enough.

Goddamn.

That's happened before.

The jeweler and I stare at each other.

Eventually I blink.

I think he thinks that means he won somehow.

So I pay and let him keep the remaining three dollars in change.

He says, "Does it ever bother you how unneeded you are, almost everywhere."

"It does," I say.

And I leave.

A few blocks from my apartment, I stop at the park.

No one else is there.

Spring will come soon.

I can tell.

Hi, hey.

Nothing will change.

Hi hey.

A squirrel runs through the tubeslide and then drinks water pooled in the tire swing.

It is funny to me.

I laugh but feel bad for some reason also.

And I take the necklace out of the bag and then hold the necklace up against the sun and the necklace looks beautiful.

I'm laughing.

I can't stop.

It's stupid-awesome.

Yes.

The laughing feels so good.

It occurs to me that there might be gum in the middle of the earth.

That makes me laugh more.

Is there gum there.

It doesn't matter.

This is so good.

And one day, there will be no evidence of me ever having lived.

No evidence identifiable.

And I've thought of no better practice.

In some dirt by the swingset, I bury the necklace.

Pretty deep for what I can do with just my fingers and the still somewhat cold ground.

Then, I'm done.

And it always seems that things are just about to drastically change and be better.

That I just have to wait.

Wait for a giant, gift-wrapped package to float to me, mine to undo.

And inside the gift-wrapped package: an endless orange and an immortal puppy and some money.

I don't know if I should judge myself based on what I can accept or what I can't accept but I do know that I always dislike where I am and then look back on where I was with sadness because it is gone.

(That means I am worthless and it's my fault.)

Ha ha!

I stand in the playground and I feel like I would never be friends with someone like myself.

Never ever.

That I would never do that.

No I don't know.

It doesn't matter.

There should be a word for what happens when you begin to ruin a feeling by saying it.

There should be less right-heres.

I wear the same clothes over and over.

I'm pretty disgusting I guess.

And in my dreams now I yell at people but make no sound.

It feels like practice.

ABOUT SAM PINK

Sam Pink is the author of The Self-Esteem Holocaust Comes Home (Lazy Fascist Press), Frowns Need Friends Too (Afterbirth Books), and I Am Going to Clone Myself Then Kill the Clone and Eat It (Paperhero Press).

Visit him online at www.impersonalelectroniccommunication.com.

CPSIA information can be obtained at www.ICGtesting.com
Printed in the USA
BVOW07s1221301214

381363BV00001B/83/P